I Live in 2 Houses

Calvin and Dad Books

Leaning Rock Press

Leaning Rock Press
Gales Ferry, CT 06335
leaningrockpress@gmail.com
www.leaningrockpress.com

CalvinandDad.com

978-1-950323-77-7: Hardcover
978-1-950323-78-4:, Softcover

Library of Congress Control Number: 2023900499

Names:	Neff, Fred, 1952- author. | Dougal, Bill, illustrator.
Title:	I live in 2 houses / [written by Fred Neff ; illustrated by Bill Dougal].
Other titles:	I live in two houses
Description:	2nd edition. | Gales Ferry, CT : Leaning Rock Press, [2023] | Series: Calvin and Dad books | Interest age level: 004-010. | Summary: Calvin's parents have divorced with Calvin dividing his time between his parent's two houses. He enjoys having different experiences with both parents who make his time with them memorable, enjoyable, and filled with love. Calvin and his dad ponder the realities of divorce as they find and share a silver lining.--Publisher.
Identifiers:	ISBN: 978-1-950323-77-7 (hardcover) | 978-1-950323-78-4 (softcover) | LCCN: 2023900499
Subjects:	LCSH: Children of divorced parents--Juvenile fiction. | Fathers and sons--Juvenile fiction. | Divorce--Juvenile fiction. | Emotions--Juvenile fiction. | CYAC: Children of divorced parents--Fiction. | Fathers and sons--Fiction. | Divorce--Fiction. | Emotions--Fiction. | LCGFT: Domestic fiction. | BISAC: JUVENILE FICTION / Family / Marriage & Divorce. | JUVENILE FICTION / Family / Parents. | JUVENILE FICTION / Social Themes / Emotions & Feelings.
Classification:	LCC: PZ7.1.N3924 Il 2023 | DDC: [E]--dc23

Printed in the United States of America

Acknowledgments

The Lord is first and foremost to thank for planting seeds of ability in me to write with a passion during good times and faith to continue my craft during the stormiest of times.

My son, Calvin, continues to inspire story material as we travel through life enjoying the fatherhood experiences created together, just being Calvin and Dad.

A little-known national program, Fatherhood Initiative, focuses on empowering dads to take a prominent role in their kids' lives. Whether boys or girls, toddlers or teens, they all need one-on-one time with Dad. Doesn't matter as much what Dad is doing so much as it includes them in the process. Kids want to be a valued part of your life, Dad. For his influence on the Calvin and Dad series, I thank the local program's director, Gabe Fonseca, who facilitated the Monday night group meetings I attended at Madonna Place, in Norwich, CT. He imparted wisdom with care and compassionate understanding, drawing out from many a father, the true dad inside.

In writing this story I attempted to strike a balance from Calvin's perspective early in the book, portraying life with Mom as well as life with Dad. Some illustrations were drawn from photos of Calvin, like 'snowboarding' a toboggan down the hillside at my house.

The idea of exclusivity with a parent, in this case alternating weekends with Dad, is reality for many children of divorced parents. As normal as the nuclear family used to be, living in two houses is becoming a reality that kids and parents alike are now having to adjust to. Like a glass of water half empty or half full, perception will most likely determine you and your child's acceptance of this arrangement.

You may be surprised like I was, that very few people of traditional households identify with the silver lining that Calvin and I enjoy in parent-child exclusivity depicted in the storyline of I Live in 2 Houses. However, whatever choices you face, remember that old fashioned hugs and kisses make love happen in every child's life, regardless of age!

Although the Friendly's Restaurant in Mystic, CT is no longer in operation, I still want to thank the staff who were there when I was writing this book. I truly felt at home there, rhyming each of my stories over breakfast and coffee.

The Author

Hi, my name is Calvin.

I live in one house

where riding my bike is neat.

My mom says that's because

we live on a dead end street.

At Mom's I run and play games.

Cars drive slow on a cul-de-sac.

They always stop and wave to me.

I smile to them and then wave back.

I also live in a house on a hill

off the road, back in the woods.

Dad teaches me outdoor stuff.

He says I learn what boys should.

I ride my pedal truck at Dad's.

I really zoom down the big hill.

He always chases after me. I laugh.

By now he knows the drill.

7

I watch my dad when he works

outside the house.

He sure works hard.

He says it's a guy's job, and that

one day I'll have my own yard.

When we rake leaves,

I get my own rake.

We make a stack,

then take a break.

Dad says the leaves are in too big a pile.

I laugh, run and jump. Dad smiles.

We work hard getting ready

for the winter season.

We rake leaves and stack wood

for good reason.

Dad says hard work must come before we play,

so we rake leaves and cart some wood today.

When it snows Mom takes me

to a Vermont chalet.

That's a fancy name

for where we always stay.

I ski there and snowboard down the hillside,

then catch the chair lift back up—it's a cool ride!

At Dad's house we don't drive to see the snow.

It comes to us, and my dad's glad when it goes.

We live where winters get cold, not just chilly.

The snow gets slippery at Dad's 'cause it's very hilly.

Dad fires up the snowblower.

I ask what I can do.

"Shovel a path

to the bird feeder,

then I'll play with you."

High on the hill I'm scared

to slide without my dad.

So at first we ride together.

It's a lot of fun we have.

Then I show Dad how I can snowboard

like when I'm with my mom.

He's scared I'll fall. And I do.

It's the way I learned with her, too.

Dad sighs . . . and says it's time,

but asks what I like best before we go.

He just smiles when I look at him

and say, "Shoveling snow."

Sliding down the slippery hill

is fun I guess,

but helping Dad around the house

is what I like best.

There are some kids I play with

whose moms live with their dads.

They wonder why I have two homes.

It's what I've always had.

Once a boy who lives on Mom's cul-de-sac

was waving to me, bye-bye.

I climbed up into Dad's big truck.

Then I looked back and saw him cry.

He wanted to come and be with us.

I know that's why he's sad.

He doesn't have a house to go to

where he can be with just his dad.

My dad also saw the boy

and had some advice to give.

He told me families

make tough choices,

sometimes in how they live.

Dad says it's not about the toys,

girls and boys, what's hers or his,

or zooming down a hill real fast,

but how much love we can give.

My dad tells me happiness

is something we cannot hide,

and doesn't start with others,

but lives way down inside.

Even when the love seems brief

and we don't get life's wishes,

Dad says love can multiply

with real big hugs and lots of kisses.

Even when our worlds may change,

love is always fashioned

after little girls and boys,

'cause we can make love happen!

Books by Fred Neff

Fatherhood as seen through the eyes of a child

The series chronicles the bond Calvin and his dad share as they explore a parade of life's marvels, some seemingly ordinary, but always humorous, and with a twist. Each story, told in first person from Calvin's perspective, allows the adult reader to chuckle over a child's perspective of how things are and reminisce of the days of Dad teaching a child, and of course, a child teaching Dad.

CALVIN and DAD Series

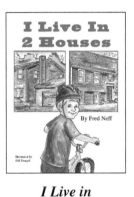

I Live in 2 Houses

As Calvin and Dad ponder the realities of divorce, they find and share a silver lining.

Pirate Calvin Meets the Wise Seaport Rat

Join young Calvin at Schooner Seaport where he takes on a pirate's dare.

The Memory Tree

This story recounts actual Christmas events. Calvin helps transform this Christmas into a tradition they will recapture for years to come.

Calvin and the Red Neck Wagon

Chuckle with Calvin as he relates firsthand this true story of building a wagon in rural Virginia. Only in the South can you build a wagon like this!

Grocery Shopping With Dad

Come along, reminisce and chuckle with Calvin as he transforms ordinary food shopping into a learning adventure with Dad.

The Great Mouse Caper

To avoid a winter food shortage at Christmas time, a clan of mice living in the attic plans a notorious caper, fooling nearly everyone.

Can Gi-Normus The Tow Truck and Squawky Palone Save Christmas?

Cheer with your child as a chatterbox fox (Squawky Palone) and a very unusual tow truck try to save Santa whose sleigh is stuck on a rooftop— on Christmas Eve!

Farnsworth the Firehose and Taylor Grief

In trying to save a little girl's dog, they are caught in the attic of a burning house, where teamwork and trust are tested to their limits in a climactic ending to this rescue series thriller!

Buddy the Ambulance and Angel Ann

Inspirational story of Buddy the Ambulance and his two EMTs, Sam and Ann, taking a critical call for help that stretches their abilities to save a little boy and his dog from certain peril at the seashore.

CPSIA information can be obtained
at www.ICGtesting.com
Printed in the USA
BVHW011613100223
658261BV00020B/110